843   CHAMOISEAU

Chamoiseau, Patrick.
Seven dreams of Elmira : a
tale of Martinique

WITHDRAWN

AUG 2 4 1999

KEEP DATE DUE CARD IN THIS POCKET

Library Card Necessary
For Checkout

The card holder is responsible
for all books drawn on his card

DODGE CITY PUBLIC LIBRARY
1001 Second Ave.
Dodge City, Kansas

Dodge City Public Library
Dodge City, Kansas

Seven Dreams of Elmira: A Tale of Martinique

Dodge City Public Library
Dodge City, Kansas

Seven Dreams of Elmira: A Tale of Martinique

Being the Confessions of an Old Worker at the Saint-Etienne Distillery

PATRICK CHAMOISEAU

Photographs by
JEAN-LUC DE LAGUARIGUE

Translated from the French by
MARK POLIZZOTTI

ZOLAND BOOKS
Cambridge, Massachusetts

2000

First English edition published in 1999 by
Zoland Books, Inc.
384 Huron Avenue
Cambridge, Massachusetts
02138

Copyright © 1999 by Patrick Chamoiseau
Photographs copyright © 1999 by Jean-Luc de Laguarigue
Translation copyright © 1999 by Mark Polizzotti

Originally published in French as *Elmire des sept bonheurs*
by Editions Gallimard, Paris, 1998.
Copyright © 1998 by Sonofa-Habitation Saint-Etienne
and Editions Gallimard.

PUBLISHER' NOTE
All rights reserved. No part of this book may be used
or reproduced in any manner whatsoever without written
permission, except in the case of brief quotations
embodied in critical articles or reviews.

05 04 03 02 01 00 99   8 7 6 5 4 3 2 1

This book is printed on acid-free paper, and its binding materials
have been chosen for strength and durability.

LIBRARY OF CONGRESS CATALOGING-IN-PUBLICATION DATA

Chamoiseau, Patrick.
[Elmire des sept bonheurs. English]
Seven dreams of Elmira : a tale of Martinique /
Patrick Chamoiseau : translated by Mark Polizzotti :
photographs by Jean-Luc de Laguarigue.
p. cm.
ISBN 1-58195-002-0
I. Polizzotti, Mark. II. Laguarigue, Jean-Luc de.
III. Title. IV. Title: 7 dreams of Elmira.
PQ3949.2.C45E4313 1999
843—dc21   98-54295
CIP

Thanks to the residents of Gros-Morne, commanders of memory, who were kind enough to share their experiences: Daniel Bavarin (p. 45), Jean-Louis Bernard (p. 37), Clothilde and Emmanuel Billard (p. 34), Hector Biron (p. 42), Mme. Bordes, Thérese and Roland Clémentine (p. 38), Emilie Corentin (p. 44), Christian Démoléon, Marcel Gaumont, Nanette and Gesner Germany (p. 39), Jean Goyette, Faustin Hébert (p. 43), Lucien Irilo (p. 48), Fanotte Languedoc, Gracieuse Languedoc (p. 40), Emma Legendard, Nonotte and Clavius Lerichard (p. 35), Julien Marie-Joseph, Apolline Mexique (p. 32), M. Morin, Félicité Mothy, Augustin Nelien, Renoir Ovarbury (p. 33), Gustave Pain, René Pavadé, Eldor Risal (p. 41), Maurice Simon, Fortuné Ténébay (p. 36), Joachim-Belisaire Vesanes (p. 49).

Many thanks to José Hayot who must have seen Elmira one day in a joyful dream, for he had no trouble awakening her in me.

—P.C.

To Shinsai, who just arrived

A century of tales float above the Saint-Etienne distillery, like clusters of bamboo in a bottomless ravine. Secrets hover there, too—a ball of secrets linking 1893 to the present. The old workers make out like they know them, but only I truly preserve them in my memory. For I have known the cutting, the hoisting, the mashing. I've brewed the ferment in the vats. I've worked the distilling column. I've seen the hot liquid being tested, put the rum in casks, and served as tilbury driver to the founding *békés*. I've seen it all. Handled it all. Heard it all. Oh, I've got loads to tell: enough to set your teeth on edge or make your heart flip. But I'll have nothing to do with the dimwitted blabbity-blah of those good-time Negroes (tongue in the breeze, head in the clouds); they know nothing of miracles, only useless facts. Many have begged at the door of my hut for the secret of that Gros-Morne rum that has made us the world's envy. They were wasting their time. I didn't tell them a goddamn thing.

It's just that telling that secret isn't even a possibility. Of course I could talk about the matchless soil of Gros-Morne, with its high yields, the seven benedictions it receives from the sun. Here, the cane is more loaded with syrup than a New Year's Eve: it's good for sugar, and even better for rum. And then you have to know how to cut that cane, talk to it as it falls, bundle it the right way, offer it to the grinders with due respect. You have to find the murmur of the wort in the long fermentation vats. And then there's the holy rite of distillation, which preserves in the spirit of the rum the mysteries of earth, grass, fruit and fine spice— everything the sugarcane absorbs as it rises toward the sky. It's an accumulation of little secrets: I know them all without knowing their heart. Every one of us who has hoed this earth, each of us over a hundred years old, owns a part of it. As if a Mama-light, opening in our memories, had seeped into our movements: an old knowledge, a true carnal knowledge that gives the rum a soul which no machine in the world could form. And so I'll go away from here without revealing a thing. I'll leave behind my yam ditches and sun-bleached mule, but I'll take with me my parcel of truth, just as Old Man Simonnet, the long-time head of the distillery, went off with his. Those who think I'm going to spill the beans can just go to sleep right now: even if I did give away my bit of the secret, the sharpest and craftiest wouldn't understand a thing without the other bits.

Legends, secrets, a thousand tales. *So many!...* Hmm, hm, hm, sometimes I just have to chuckle to myself. I'm thinking of Zolbè the gravedigger (who pushed the hand-trucks) begging the priest the bury him right in the soil next to his hut, and who, all stiff and dead as he was, spread his arms in a *Long-Live-de Gaulle* to keep from going into his poor-man's coffin. When they finally managed to stuff him in there, he swelled up with such rage that the coffin split apart like a custard apple. The priest had to give in and bury him the way he wanted, in the blissful clay of the Gros-Morne that bathes our plantations. Hmm, hmm, hm.

I'm thinking of Théolomène the sorcerer, who used to work with the fertilizer. He had conjured up a something-or-other to hold off the dry season and that something-or-other came in the form of a blaze on the seventh stroke of midnight that burnt down his hut, broad knife, chickens, rabbits, dishes, shed, and himself, Théolomène, standing in the middle of all that with his arms folded at the spectacle of his own consumption. We scurried around him with our hearts in our throats, throwing water, throwing sand— not to save Théolomène, Hmm, hm, hm… but so the fire wouldn't reach the dry straw of our cane.

I'm thinking of that poor devil we saw coming from the woods in the middle of the harvest season. He was covered in mushrooms and a shirt of vines. No one knew him from Adam, not at Gros-Morne nor anywhere else on the Caribbean earth. The Stranger wanted a sugarcane to suck on come hell or high water *(just one Saint-Etienne cane!…)*

before going back to wherever he came from, to that place no reality could convey. He seemed sad as a sea urchin. He spoke a Creole from the depths of memory, the kind only a long-gone-ancient (forgotten by death) could claim to recognize, Hmm, hm, hmm…

I'm also thinking about evenings after the cutting, when exhaustion sent us staggering back to our huts, and about that she-devil who suddenly appeared from the edge of the Man Roi cliff. She came white on a white mule, slowly climbing arse-backward up the cliffside. Clippityclop clippityclop clippityclop. She didn't look sad or lost or abandoned; she just wore the deathless solitude of immortals, and a spectral boredom. The old ones had seen her, and the old ones' old ones warned each new generation of our distillery workers about her in every age of our distillery. And still, every time she appeared, everyone found himself with his heart in his throat, Hmmm… Clippityclop clippityclop clippityclop.

I'm also thinking about Colocomède, that big teddy bear of a man. He was a good mason. All by himself he had built the reinforced cement smokestack that scatters the steam of Saint-Etienne above the bluffs like a victory palm. A good mason, but he had a sweet tooth. In the middle of the harvest he threw himself on a hand-truck full of our sugarcane stalks to swallow them whole, without even really chewing. He would have wolfed down the whole thing if I hadn't grabbed him by the Adam's apple, Hmm, hm, hm...

I'm thinking, oh I'm thinking about Mam Amélya Sérénise, a good, simple woman who worked her whole life washing vats and then doing the bottling. One of those days-not-to-be-believed, we saw her wake up, get dressed as if for Palm Sunday, take a very pretty bouquet of hibiscus and two bottles of our Saint-Etienne, and walk with a determined step toward a place in the depths of the woods from where no one in the world would see her return. Old Man Simonnet didn't even cry for her—as he said, with two good bottles you take along your own Heaven, even behind the Good Lord's back, Hmmm, hm, hm...

I'm thinking about Pè Dèdè, who drove the tractor with its big wheels that came from France. He was the only one in Gros-Morne who could treat snakebite. He guarded the secret of his medicine so tightly that he finally took it with him to the grave, without a sigh, without regrets, but also without managing to hide the fact that his power against the Beast contained a few drops of our Saint-Etienne. Hmm, hm, hm, I'm thinking, I'm thinking...

A load of small, laughable things that we lived with around the distillery. They blended with the noises of the boiler, the blasts of steam that streaked the countryside, the fragrance of the rum spirits that made the cane mash bubble. I still live with those thoughts: they bring back a life of labor and crown my memory, laden with the heady aroma of the first cane flowers.

Life becomes cheap when you pass a hundred. The sun doesn't fill you with wonder anymore, not even when it rises above the pear trees, in the fog off the red lands of Tracée, Deux-Terres, Bois-d'Inde, Dumaine, Bois-Lézard, or Glottin, where the nutmeg trees are so rich that the leaves explode in blue bursts amid the green. No more wonder, just an expectation beyond desire. We feel it when we—the old workers from this plantation—gather around a bowl of punch made with our rum. Then we climb Morne-Calvaire to look down on the expanse of our Gros-Morne: to see it spread toward Fonds-Saint-Denis, Marigot, Sainte-Marie; see it extend in an abundance of breadfruit trees and litchis toward La Trinité and Le Robert; see it fall toward Lamentin and Saint-Joseph in purple swathes of sugarcane, mango trees, and well-raked lawns. From that height, it's a joy to see the smoke-stack of our distillery in the blowing trade winds, the herky-jerky of its century-old machines, the anthill of its trucks heading off to deliver our nectar, which makes distillers throughout the Caribbean weep tears of respectful rage.

Yes, this is what remains. This distillery, this rum: we're the ones who made it, all of us together, each one under the weight of his poverty, each with his own secret that is linked to the secret of the Earth. It makes us laugh to see the new workers puff up their chests over the incomparable brilliance of our rum: they still think *they* have something to do with it. But there's a century of other lives in there; a century of patience, work, and intelligence; a grace that reaches beyond vanity. We gather together like this, fewer and fewer with every burial. Each of us promising the others that nothing, not the police and not the clergy, will stop him from slipping a bottle of Saint-Etienne into the crate of his last journey, and three drops in the incense, and seven more in the holy water—enough to let him walk toward the other side with a valiant heart and his soul in the right place, and especially with the one absence we all share: *Elmira!...*

Elmira of the seven splendors and every grace.
She's the one I wanted to talk about.

Isidore Adélodaine saw her first. He was a kind of simpleton to whom Old Man Simonnet had given a simpleton's chores: taking care of the garden, pruning the plants, hauling the manure, picking up the cane trash, and other insignificant tasks he handled with a seriousness that made him seem almost normal. Isidore was the first to discover the celestial Queen of our rum, not because his taste buds were keener but just because of his *greater innocence.* Every season, we would gather around the first distillate at 160 proof. Old Man Simonnet was there, wearing his gold watch, but he wasn't alone. There were also the Aubéry-ghosts who had owned the distillery at its origins; they stood milky-white near the wine heater, alongside other *béké* ancestors who looked like pirates. The shadows of the machines shimmered with all the souls who had worked there before: the ones who'd kept the books in the plantation grocery; the ones who'd cut eternities of sugarcane; the ones who'd bundled it; the ones who'd worn out hand-trucks and carts carrying it; who'd tamed the red brilliance of the forge; who'd made the steam boiler rumble; who'd kept the hydraulic mill running under the fury of the canals; who'd directed the raising of the pulley; the masons; the carpenters; the mechanics; the coopers; the ones who filled the vats and the ones who filled the bottles; the accountants and foremen; the managers and tilbury drivers; the ox-herders and mule-keepers, big blabbermouths on Saturday payday; the drainage-tank workers; the newly arrived *koulis,* housed across the river, who nobody went to see; the master-distillers who orchestrated the spirit of our rum in the chaudfroid of the coils. *All those people!...* The population of Saint-Etienne down through the ages came together like that, around the first droplets pearling in the copper kettle. Even a few souls who didn't belong to the plantation watched the ritual: prisoners under police guard who'd stopped off on our property before being delivered to Saint-Joseph; men and women who drifted in from the four corners of the country, because once in their lives (unforgettable!...) they had tasted our rum; those who had heard tell of it; those who wanted to know what it was like; the Syrians who'd crisscrossed the commune with their wheelbarrows; the Chinese grocers who'd sold the rum bit by bit in corner stores; the former mayors of Gros-Morne—Thaly, Vautor, Nazair and Maugée—who still maintained their chauvinistic pride.... All those people, all those people coming from the exiles of life.

We didn't find that crowd of zombies especially comforting, but even so we could feel they were benevolent, like the thousand-year-old trees scattered over the fields.

And so: the annual anxiety over the first droplets. Had our rum lost its magic? Had some old Negro medium cast an evil spell on our cane? Had some mishap of sun or earth ruined the splendors of its flavor? Had some bitterness in the column damaged its aftertaste? We tasted it with those fears in our hearts. I said *tasted,* not guzzled. You put a drop on the palm of your hand, rub it hard, and breathe it in fast to catch the scent of a possible misfortune unawares. Then, eyes closed, you let the second droplet coat your tongue, reach your eyes, then spread the full array of its succulence through your head. That's how we did it. That year, one of my very first, everyone was happy. We cried out, *Woulo!* The rum had gone beyond good: it careened into those raptures that the master-distillers acknowledge by saying, *Yeah Yeah Yeah.* Well, Isidore Adélodaine the simpleton, instead of saying *Yeah Yeah Yeah,* began to murmur, both eyes staring at some creature unseen by the rest of the gathering, even by those who could make out the zombies from the distillery's first century, ghosts who know every gasket, every chain. The simpleton glimpsed something more. Then he saw nothing. Desperate, he begged for just one more drop, and again he saw what he had seen, which appeared to make him happy: not the joys of an unfettered rummy or the psychiatries of buggers-who-see-pink-elephants, but a happiness-glow radiating from within.

Ho, the simpleton was trembling easy!

Suddenly he saw nothing more, and all his weight settled back into his drooling flesh; his gaze became unsteady, blinded by memories. No way to make him tell what he'd seen. He held his secret close like the hiding place of a treasure. He tried to recapture his ecstasy with rum stolen from the warehouse, which he swallowed without periods or commas. Rum demands measure, and measure gives the fullness of taste. A rum punch takes a good six hours to penetrate a soul. Six hours, between the midday punch that wards off the sun's madness and the punch before your evening soup, the commander of your dreams. But he, the simpleton, could no longer wait for that fruitful crossing. From glass to glass he chased after his ephemeral bliss. But what he had seen wouldn't return, and so he overdid it. We found him at the foot of the kapok tree, uprooted by raving rum, howling over the lost vision without which his life was now just dead wood.

I went to see him with two cronies one Sunday. Just before the mass in town so he could reveal to us, on an empty stomach, what the Saint-Etienne had shown him. We were expecting sinister marvels: the bloody path to some Dutch pirate treasure, the whereabouts of a Provençal jar bursting with gold and jewels under a pyramid of bones. We dreaded the prophetic nightmare of a leper or some other dangerous calamity. Using signs (the burden of simpleness had blocked his throat), he told us only that he'd seen someone. Just someone. That that someone was one of those dramatically beautiful matadors who open an unbridgeable gap in your life. The human being is incomplete. I know this: I'm more than one hundred years old and still I'm not fulfilled. You make do as best you can with a few tricks and two or three false passions, but you remain incomplete, unfinished like those barren plum trees yellowing in distress. Faced with that creature, the simpleton had a vision of something that had always been lost to him. He heard his own voice, which he knew nothing about; he became aware of his words, lost in a ditch deep within himself. What happened to him worried us: for a woman to arouse such emotions in that innocent flesh meant she was more than just special. We tried to see her ourselves, without really expecting to. That day we forgot all about mass. In the empty distillery, sitting near the coils, we invoked the Divinity with bowls of punch made from our rum. To take Saint-Etienne in your mouth, follow its detonation inside your cheeks, dream its slow flight throughout your body. Then wait. Our rum had reached wicked heights. We could feel it. We were living it. But we didn't see a thing. Sometimes we devined a volatile presence in the ether of tastes, but still there was no creature.

Suddenly, Paulo Atéthonase began to talk gibberish.

To talk gibberish the way you talk gibberish in the face of the unseeable.

A surplus of life. Something outside reality that leaves

you, not terrified, but dependent forevermore. *He saw the creature.* He spoke to her in words from a language that was not proud. He walked toward her. He wanted to touch her. She seemed to treat him with kindness, gave him a smile, a caress with her eyes, a generous gesture that, in dissipating, left our Paulo like a man abandoned by the Earth itself, waking alone on the burning rock of the Savane des Pétrifications.

We brought him back home. There, we first had to hold him down to keep him from guzzling entire bottles in search of the Young Lady. Shrouded in his blissful memory, he managed to speak of her. I say "speak," but that's not really it. He tried to *evoke* her. It was a difficult thing. She was a kind of high yellow, but also quadroon, but also mulatress, but also *koulie*, but also Caribbean, but also Negress, vaguely Chinese and Syrian, a variable beauty, fluid like the ocean lifting its acclamations to the sky. She wore the twisted plaid head scarf of old Saint-Pierre tradition, embellished with a brooch and a pin. A short-sleeved blouse of embroidered white cotton, threaded through with lace and red satin. A full pleated skirt raised over a mocking hip, and an underskirt of velvet or alchemical silk. He saw she was wearing sandals with embroidered uppers and white lisle socks rolled down at the ankles. He saw her bare throat with its necklace of gold beads. He saw her eyes shining like a *bois-canon* leaf before a rainstorm. Her thick, thick hair billowed from her plaid headdress down to her Creole earrings. And then she smiled. Not some little pucker of earthly sympathy, but an enveloping, magnetic smile, as in the time of the great rains. She was woman, mama, matador, saint, haughty, marvelous, a tabernacle of hungry lives…. That was how Paulo described her, all unglued as he was, following the demands of the far-flung zones of his mind and the wounds life had inflicted on him. We peered around us, trying to see her. Some had another glass of Saint-Etienne right then and there. But they experienced only the ritual pleasure. The girl was capricious. Not at just any moment, and not with just anyone. You had to deserve her, according to rules our lawbooks and our bibles did not recognize.

The apparition became a great secret: in other words, it spread from confidence to confidence, from one ear to the next. Which caused the workers, the boiler cleaners, the valve regulators, the bottle carriers, the vat washers, the mash stirrers, the basin drainers—everyone, at noon and at around five in the evening, to sit with pounding hearts before a few fingers of Saint-Etienne. Everyone prepared his punch with tragic hopes. Everyone practiced the silent turn of the wrist, the offering to the lips, the absorption of the nectar with its ceremony of precious gestures. And everyone waited. There were countless disappointments. No one saw anything, though from year's end to year's end not a day went by without some joker boasting of having had a vision. But none of them could describe anything more than somber idiocies or the uniquely pleasurable rites of our rum. The Young Lady had to be deserved, and the chosen were few.

The simpleton waited for her for more than sixty years. Even on the day of his death, at the age of ninety-five, he was still hoping.

At the final stage of his death agony, we offered him his punch. Behind the priest's back, we sanctified his holy water with seven drops of our rum. In his coffin, we slipped a bottle according to our pagan laws, urging the Young Lady to please visit him on the other side.

As for Paulo Atéthonase, he never saw her again. White-haired, weary of living, he yearned for the mist where that apparition could be found. But his daily bowls of punch gave him so many papaya-hopes of seeing her again that he ended up staying among us for a long time. It was on the day of his death (at the age of 123 years, six months, three days, seven hours, four minutes, and three seconds—not so very long ago), drinking his final punch, that he named her in a last sigh. I was the only one to hear it: his face suddenly looked contented; his eyes fixed on a marvelous brilliance; his lip curled onto something unutterable. Leaning over his deathbed I heard his joyful murmur, *Elmira...* Yes, that was it, I think: *Elima*, or *Elyra*, or *Elrima*. But since those names don't really exist, I believe our Young Lady must be called Elmira.

Then, as the years passed, other workers saw her as well. Each apparition widened the circle of the woman's admirers. Elmira came to them just when they had stopped thinking about her, sitting with their bottle of Saint-Etienne to puzzle out life, hearts light, eyes gazing without greed on the world, bodies at rest, heads free, their feet planted flat on the ground of Gros-Morne, their fingers still encrusted with clay, skinned by arrogant cane stalks, not yet soaped and scented, connected in some way to the whole of the plantation. She visited them as they brought the glass to their pensive lips, when the rum in an imperceptible fusion became one with their entire being. At that moment, the world took on a decisive, petrifying, liberating brilliance. An uncommonly gentle authority. And then they saw Elmira.

Elmira traveled on the hand-carts that delivered the kegs; and later, on the trucks delivering the bottles. Ecstatic men and illuminated women began arriving from all over: from Saint-Joseph, Macouba, Grand-Rivière, and Fonds-

Moustique; from the far depths of Trinité; from Derrière-Morne to Sainte-Marie; from the old Cape of Saint Anne. We saw some who came from Marie-Galante, Saint Lucia, or Barbados, and others who found their way from Poland and Iceland, where our bottles had washed ashore. They arrived like pilgrims forever lost within their memories, or like apostles announcing an enchantment, or like the prophets of an intimate paradise. They spoke in muffled voices, eyes lowered for fear they'd be taken for plumb lunatics. They entered the Saint-Etienne plantation as if it were the promised land, a kind of sanctuary they had lost in themselves and rediscovered here. No need to speak or look us in the eye. Seeing them approach like blind moons, ill and exalted from an irreparable loss, we welcomed them with envious kindness. We told them in conspiratorial tones that they'd had the impossible good fortune of seeing the Young Lady. They merely wanted to know her name. We told them: *Elmira.*

One of them moaned, *Elmira of the seven splendors.*

Another sighed, *Elmira of every grace and other delights.*

Then they went away again, murmuring those phrases in the pit of their stomachs, convinced that if they called her that way she would reappear at some unhoped-for moment in the rest of their lives.

One day, a painter arrived from who knows where. He

had found a bottle of our Saint-Etienne on a boat that ran aground near Maripasoula, in Guyana, in the depths of the jungle, among the baboons and anacondas. He had drunk it in the company of Ndjuka maroons and Wayampi Indians at the foot of the sacred mountain. And, by a harrowing stroke of luck, they had all glimpsed Elmira at the same moment, but in various ways. Elmira smiling at them, and even (but this part I don't believe) Elmira speaking to them, in a voice that can't be reproduced in writing. The brown Negroes took her for a force of Africa coming to claim them; the American Indians made her into an aquatic grace, guardian of abundance. Our painter thought she had emerged from the chimerical painting he'd been seeking in himself through-out his hopeless exile in those primordial lands. He would not rest until he could locate the distillery, ask us questions. Have us tell him about Elmira, her birth, her life, her loves, her death. He found dozens of people who had seen the Young Lady without daring to speak of her. Each described her in his way:

> for the somber of heart she was a sun;
> for the arid, a September rain shower;
> for the sick, a breath of health;
> for the condemned, a promise of life.

A writer from the French Academy thought he discerned in her a flash of poetic brilliance....

These witnesses endowed her with every kind of smile, eyes, hair. Elmira was pieced together in different ways, depending on the place, the time, the drinker, his sufferings and joys. The painter (holed up behind the huge barrels where the old rum ruminated) spent the rest of his life trying to recapture her face in a pastel stroke, or in paint. His sketches sailed over the steam boilers like orphaned leaves. His tears of dismay rusted the barrels and dissolved his gouaches. To paint that enchantment he invoked unknown colors, mixed cane juice with earth, and hot liquid with the rust of the tall vats. He crushed the tears of *manicou*-possums and the eggs of *anoli*-lizards into the blue of his mirages. He started faces, then no longer dared finish them. We soon saw him make do with a lip, an eye, the outline of a nostril or an eyebrow, reproduced over and over again. We saw him trying with reddened eyes to capture and harmonize luminous vibrations with shadowy depths. He tried out rhythms shattered by black, gray, and green; he ruined himself in geometric flashes unknown to this world; he risked himself on summits of acute sensations that pushed him into working on ten sketches at a time. He knew spirals of lucid intoxication and unctuous lucidity. I saw his hand, in a drunken dance, exhaust the lyrical distortions, artless grotesqueries, mineral densities, and crystalline transparencies of the geysers of his drama. He used materials colored by an inner power, sparkles of rock, waves of metal, shimmers of glass, respirations of hair between birth and thirty-years-in-the-grave. He wanted to be a jeweler, ceramist, glassblower, varnisher, rugweaver, potter, musician in Germanic splendor, and he was all those things on certain moons when we heard him cough out his Byzantine concentrations beside the embers firing the boilers.

One day, during a cyclone, he disappeared into a mix of gouache, grease, chalk, and pastel brought about by a depression in his desires. I don't know if it's a good death for a painter to disappear into the abyss of an unimaginable canvas, but in his case it was the only possible way out. Old Man Simonnet found in the chaos he left behind a sketched study that was slightly more finished than the rest. We all agreed the drawing should be affixed to our bottles. There was some malice involved, for those who know why we did it aren't saying, and those who don't know see that study of Elmira simply as a design on a label, without recognizing in it the prophecy of an enchantment that might catch anyone by surprise, during any bowl of rum punch and while leading any kind of life, for the most incalculable of eternities.

I have my bottles. I stare at the labels and I imagine Elmira after my own fashion. Of my generation, I am among those who never saw her. I am lacking something. No doubt some degree of innocence. Perhaps I don't have the exact number of white hairs on my loony-head. Probably I still don't mix my punch just right: not the right dose of rum, or the right gestures, or the right bit of lemon. But I am patience itself. Every day I spend an hour preparing my Saint-Etienne. I sit ceremoniously before my hut looking at the benevolent kapok tree. I listen to the song of the river Lézarde running through the plantation, from the Zoumba basin to the Désir basin, where a hand-truck and an ox vanished, from the Fourchette basin to the Tambi basin, where some *koulis* drowned. A little rum in my hand. I rub my arms with it, my neck, my face as I did when I worked the steam boiler, when I thought water was bad for you. Then I bring the glass to my lips with the feeling that sooner or later Elmira will come. That Elmira will carry me from this world toward a boundless joy. And if she doesn't carry me away, I'll go by myself—having seen her—on an idea approaching joy. The painter (I learned this only fifty years later) allowed me to understand that Elmira was in each of us, between consciousness and unconsciousness, where the maps of flesh and spirit come together to suggest to each of us the *impossibility* of our lives, its trace of elevation, the star of plenitude by which we set our art, our voice, every gesture of our existence. We are all children in that regard. Gros-Morne lifts the richness of its soil above our ruined dreams. The distillery stands here, smoking out its challenges and tallying them up as it has for so many years. In that exasperating wait, in the embers of hope and despair that guide our will, we strive, in moderation, to live as best we can; and as Elmira suggests, we try—with difficult desires, at the highest degree of impossibility—to find our quiet happiness.

42

Take landscapes unawares. Understand them.
Lead divination with an innocent gaze. Pace (above the
tangible map of light and shadow) along traces and details
that are like memoirs. What we have done remains here,
in these run-down woods, these walls weighed down with
age and daydreams, these machine angles beside which
so many have nurtured their hopes; in these barrels and
doors, and in these plantation groceries. Every distillery is
a monument. Precious fragility. Intangible loss.

What does the wall say, beneath its crown of ferns?
You are hailed by the shadows.

*Shadows and rust make their way, compact and dense. Grease links traces
of mute hands (and conscientious sweat).*

Silence is gathered to the sounds of metal. Age, rust, and paint acquire a trembling of skin. Presences.

Whitewash retains a memory of light, of lives swallowed whole.
And courage is cradled in the folds (keep them stiff).

Eternities ruminate in jailers' alliances. Alchemy pushes you toward dreams.
Patience settles in.

Through here the world opens onto marvels and mysteries. Vertigo is palpable (and dominion near at hand, in the open pages of a notebook).